DISNEY'S THE LION KING

NO WORRIES

A NEW STORY ABOUT SIMBA

By Justine Korman

Illustrated by Don Williams and H. R. Russell

A GOLDEN BOOK • NEW YORK

Western Publishing Company, Inc., Racine, Wisconsin 53404

"Ai-yeeee!" shouted Pumbaa the warthog. He slipped on a banana peel and crashed into Timon the meerkat.

"Are you both all right?" asked Simba.

Timon dug himself out of the pile of beetle shells, leaves, and dirt. "Fine," he snapped. "Just a few bruises."

Pumbaa grunted. "Sorry, Timon. Those peels get me every time," he said.

Simba looked at the mess around him. "I guess we should clean a little," he said with a sigh.

Timon gasped. "Have you already forgotten *hakuna matata*? No worries and no work!" he said. "Let's move instead. You know what they say—the bugs are always fatter on the other hill."

"Yeah!" said Simba. "Why clean when you can move?"

So the three friends set off to look for a new home. Before long, they found a tree with nice thick branches.

"There's nothing like a nap in a tree," said Simba.

Timon scrambled up the trunk. "You're right," he said. "This is nice."

"Grr-unt-unt-unt," huffed poor Pumbaa. "A little high for me to climb."

"No problem, Pumbaa," said Timon. "We'll find a place on the ground."

Soon the friends came to a cave.

"It's kind of small," said Pumbaa as they scrambled inside.

"Pumbaa, you're going to have to eat less," grumbled Timon.

Simba pushed Timon's bony elbow away from his stomach and said, "Timon, you're going to have to wiggle less."

"All right, all right. Let's keep looking," suggested Timon.

The friends found a larger cave, which they thought was perfect—until they realized they weren't alone.

"L-let's go clean up our old p-place now," Simba suggested.

"Is a brave lion like you scared of a few bats?" asked Timon.

"I'm not afraid of anything!" said Simba.

Timon shrugged. "*Hakuna matata*, my friend," he said. "I'm sure we'll find a home soon."

The friends walked until their mouths were as dry as deserts.

"This is worse than cleaning up," moaned Simba. Timon was too tired to disagree.

Pumbaa sniffed the air. "I smell water!" he shouted.

Soon the three friends were drinking water from a stream.

Timon stuffed his cheeks with chubby bugs. "Didn't I tell you? The bugs really *are* fatter on the next hill!" he said.

"Ah—nothing beats a mud bath!" exclaimed Pumbaa.

Then Simba spotted a large hollow log. "Look!" he shouted.

Timon rushed over to inspect the log. "Hey! It's perfect," he said. "Pumbaa-a-a!" he called. "I've found the perfect home!"

Simba growled.

Timon shrugged. "I mean, *we've* found the perfect home."

Pumbaa lumbered out of the stream, climbed inside the log, and was snoring within minutes. Timon stretched himself across Pumbaa's soft belly.

"Maybe we should move the log away from the water," suggested Simba.

Timon yawned. "There you go again, worrying about things that haven't happened yet. Good night, my friend. *Hakuna matata*."

"Right. No worries," said Simba. Soon he was asleep.

Simba woke to feel the log rushing toward a noise louder than a lion's roar. The friends were being pulled downstream toward a waterfall.

"Wake up!" Simba cried.

Timon's eyes snapped open. "Help! Help!" he cried. "We're doomed!"

"What about 'no worries'?" demanded Simba.

Up ahead was a tree root.

Simba lunged at it, dug in his claws, and pulled with all his might against the powerful current. The log edged closer to shore.

"Jump!" commanded Simba.

Timon leaped onto the riverbank while Simba held
the log steady.

"Come on, Pumbaa!" Timon shouted.

Pumbaa jumped.

But before Timon and Pumbaa could grab the log
and help Simba, the root snapped in two.

The current pulled the log back into the rushing
river. In seconds, Simba was lost in a whirl of water.

The next thing Simba knew, someone was jumping
on his back and water was squirting out of his mouth.

"Whew! For a moment we thought we'd lost you,
kid," Timon said. "But I saved you."

Pumbaa grunted. After all, he was the one who had
gotten his hair wet in the rescue. Timon had only
shouted directions.

"Okay, so I told Pumbaa to save you. Same thing,"
Timon added. "Anyway, *hakuna matata*—right, kid?"

But Simba wasn't so sure.

"I think we should go home and clean up now," said Simba after he caught his breath. "It's a nice home and it's worth working for. Okay?"

So the friends went back home and cleaned out the empty beetle shells and stale banana peels. After all, Timon realized, that was a lot easier than arguing with a lion!